ATTACK OF THE
TYRANNOSAURUS

DINOSAUR COVE™

ATTACK OF THE TYRANNOSAURUS

BY
REX STONE

ILLUSTRATED BY
MIKE SPOOR

SCHOLASTIC INC.
New York Toronto London Auckland Sydney
Mexico City New Delhi Hong Kong Buenos Aires

SPECIAL THANKS TO JANE CLARKE

TO THE REAL JAMIE MORGAN, WITH LOVE AND KISSES

ISBN-13: 978-0-545-05377-8
ISBN-10: 0-545-05377-3

12 11 10 9 8 7 6 5 4 3   8 9 10 11 12 13/0

Printed in the U.S.A.
First printing, May 2008

FACT FILE

JAMIE HAS JUST MOVED FROM THE CITY TO LIVE IN THE LIGHTHOUSE IN DINOSAUR COVE. JAMIE'S DAD IS OPENING A DINOSAUR MUSEUM ON THE BOTTOM FLOOR OF THE LIGHTHOUSE. WHEN JAMIE GOES HUNTING FOR FOSSILS IN THE CRUMBLING CLIFFS ON THE BEACH HE MEETS A LOCAL BOY, TOM, AND THE TWO DISCOVER AN AMAZING SECRET: A WORLD WITH REAL, LIVE DINOSAURS! SOME DINOSAURS TURN OUT TO BE FRIENDLY, BUT OTHERS ARE FEROCIOUS. . .AND HUNGRY!

JAMIE

- FULL NAME: JAMIE MORGAN
- AGE: 8 YEARS
- SIZE: 1 JATOM*
- TOP SPEED: 7 MPH
- LIKES: FOSSIL HUNTING AND LEARNING ABOUT DINOSAURS
- DISLIKES: BEING STUCK INDOORS

Jamie's eye

Jamie's foot

Jamie's hand

*NOTE: A JATOM IS THE SIZE OF JAMIE OR TOM: 4 FT TALL AND 60 LBS IN WEIGHT

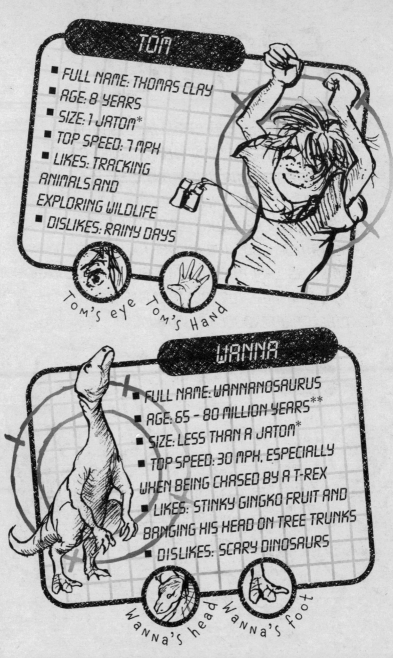

TOM

- FULL NAME: THOMAS CLAY
- AGE: 8 YEARS
- SIZE: 1 JATOM*
- TOP SPEED: 7 MPH
- LIKES: TRACKING ANIMALS AND EXPLORING WILDLIFE
- DISLIKES: RAINY DAYS

Tom's eye Tom's Hand

WANNA

- FULL NAME: WANNANOSAURUS
- AGE: 65 – 80 MILLION YEARS**
- SIZE: LESS THAN A JATOM*
- TOP SPEED: 30 MPH, ESPECIALLY WHEN BEING CHASED BY A T-REX
- LIKES: STINKY GINGKO FRUIT AND BANGING HIS HEAD ON TREE TRUNKS
- DISLIKES: SCARY DINOSAURS

Wanna's head Wanna's foot

*NOTE: A JATOM IS THE SIZE OF JAMIE OR TOM: 4 FT TALL AND 60 LBS IN WEIGHT
**NOTE: SCIENTISTS CALL THIS PERIOD THE LATE CRETACEOUS

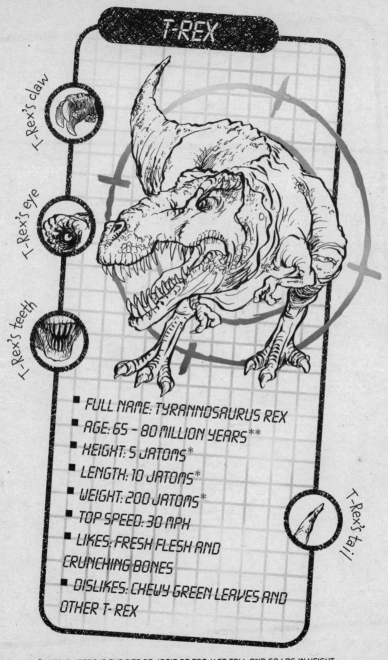

T-REX

T-Rex's claw

T-Rex's eye

T-Rex's teeth

T-Rex's tail

- FULL NAME: TYRANNOSAURUS REX
- AGE: 65 – 80 MILLION YEARS**
- HEIGHT: 5 JATOMS*
- LENGTH: 10 JATOMS*
- WEIGHT: 200 JATOMS*
- TOP SPEED: 30 MPH
- LIKES: FRESH FLESH AND CRUNCHING BONES
- DISLIKES: CHEWY GREEN LEAVES AND OTHER T-REX

*NOTE: A JATOM IS THE SIZE OF JAMIE OR TOM: 4 FT TALL AND 60 LBS IN WEIGHT

**NOTE: SCIENTISTS CALL THIS PERIOD THE LATE CRETACEOUS

Landslips where
clay and fossils are

High tide beach line

Low tide beach line

Sea

DINO CAVE

Smugglers' Point

"**D**inosaur Cove!" Jamie ran to the cliff's edge and looked down over the fence. "This has got to be the best place on Earth to find dinosaurs!"

His grandfather's eyes twinkled. "They're down there in the rocks, that's for sure. Why don't you go and have a look?"

"Fossils, here I come!" Jamie said. "See you later, Grandpa."

Jamie scrambled down the rocky path from the old lighthouse onto the sand. He turned away from the sea and ran straight up the beach,

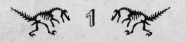

over pebbles and rocks, to the sludgy black mud nearest the foot of the cliff.

That was the place to find fossils.

Jamie kept his eyes fixed on the muddy rocks and every so often he bent down to pick one up. They were crumbly and broke apart in his fingers, but none of them had a fossil inside. *Maybe I should try a bigger rock*, he thought.

He spotted a large blue-gray rock with a crack down the middle and dumped his backpack on the mud beside it. He dug out his safety goggles, fossil hammer, and chisel. Then he set to work, angling the chisel into the crack and

tapping it with his hammer. He tapped again. This time, he tapped harder.

A stone chip pinged off Jamie's goggles as the rock split cleanly in two.

"Treasure!" Jamie said.

Sticking out of one half of the rock was a black spiral fossil with shiny gold ridges. He looked at it closely. It was about the length of his finger. But when he tried to pick it out, it didn't budge. It was stuck in the rock.

The Fossil Finder will tell me what it is, Jamie

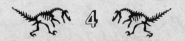

thought. He fished in his backpack and took out his favorite new gadget — a hand-held computer. He flipped the lid, and the screen glowed with a picture of a fossilized dinosaur footprint, then the words: *HAPPY HUNTING!*

At the bottom of the screen, a cursor blinked. Jamie tapped *FOSSIL SHELL* on the small keypad, looked again at his fossil, and typed what it looked like: *COILED ROPE*. Then he pressed *FIND* and stared at the screen. A picture

popped up. It looked just like the fossil in the blue-gray rock.

AMMONITE, Jamie read. *A FOSSIL SHELL FROM A PREHISTORIC SEA CREATURE, COMMON IN ROCKS FROM DINOSAUR TIMES; CAN BE FORMED OF FOOLS GOLD.*

He flipped the lid shut.

"Well," Jamie said to his discovery, "I don't care that you're common, or that you're not real gold. You come from dinosaur times, and I'm the first person ever to see you. So you're still treasure to me!"

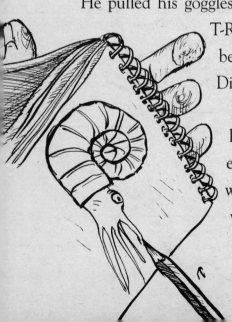

He pulled his goggles off, took out his new T-Rex notebook, and began to sketch his first Dinosaur Cove discovery. He added in the squid-like tentacles and big eyes that the creature would have had when it was alive.

Suddenly, an unfamiliar voice shouted,
"BOO!"

A freckly face popped up from behind the rock. "Gotcha! You didn't hear me coming, did you?" The boy stood up. His T-shirt and safari shorts were plastered in mud. "Is that the new Fossil Finder?"

Jamie smiled and patted the lid. "Latest software and everything."

The boy pushed his curly red hair behind his sticky-out ears. "I'm Tom Clay," he said. "I'm learning to track animals and I'm going to be a wildlife presenter on TV one day. Who are you?"

"Jamie Morgan," said Jamie. "I want to be a scientist."

"You're new, aren't you?" Tom asked.

Jamie nodded. "I just moved here. Look! I found an ammonite."

"Oh, ammonites," said Tom, shrugging. "You'll find loads of those around here."

"I want to find a dinosaur bone," Jamie told him. "Dinosaurs are awesome!"

Tom looked at Jamie's notebook and laughed. "T-Rex rules!" He put his binoculars to his

eyes. "Sometimes I pretend
I'm tracking dinosaurs. . . ."
His binoculars flashed in
the sunshine as he turned
them on Jamie.

Tom grinned. "Hey, do you want
to know a secret about Dinosaur Cove?"

"You bet!" said Jamie.

"Then follow me. We have to be quick!"
Tom set off across the beach.

Jamie stuffed his fossil-hunting gear into his
backpack and ran after his new friend. "Why
are we hurrying?" Jamie asked.

"The path up the cliff gets cut off at high
tide," Tom said. "So we'll have to get back
before then."

Tom led Jamie onto a narrow path up
a cliff, and at the highest point on the
path, Jamie stopped to look at the view. He
could see his grandfather fishing down on the
beach.

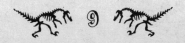

"That's my house," Jamie told Tom, pointing to the tall white-washed tower at the top of the cliffs on the opposite side of the beach.

Tom looked surprised. "The captain's lighthouse?"

"The captain is my grandpa," Jamie explained. "My dad moved us down here and he's turning the bottom floor into a dinosaur museum."

"Cool!" said Tom. He turned to look at the huge pile of mossy boulders. "We've got to get up there."

"I love climbing!" Jamie said.

Together the boys clambered up the boulders. Once Jamie had hauled himself onto the huge stone at the top, he asked, "So, where's the big secret?"

"Right behind you," Tom told him.

Jamie spun around. Behind the boulder and hidden from the bay was the gaping mouth of a cave.

"A secret cave!" Jamie gasped.

CHAPTER 2

"It's a smugglers' cave," Tom told Jamie. "It hasn't been used for a hundred years."

Jamie stepped into the mouth of the dark cave and dug his hand into his backpack, pulling out his flashlight.

"This is where the smugglers stored their booty," Tom said. "You can see the marks from their lamps."

Jamie flicked on his flashlight and pointed it toward the pale rock walls. He could make out

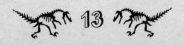

sooty black streaks. Tom took a few more steps into the cave and knocked on the back wall. "It's a dead end."

Jamie shone his flashlight over the floor and saw a spider with long, spindly legs. He followed it with the beam as it skittered into the corner and then disappeared into a hole.

"It can't be a dead end," Jamie said. "Look!"

The hole began at the cave floor and came

up to the height of his knees. It was wide at the bottom, but very narrow at the top.

"How did I miss that?" Tom said. "I've been in here loads of times."

"It's big enough to squeeze through." Jamie kneeled down and pushed his backpack through the gap. "I'm going in." He wriggled through the gap, shining his flashlight into the darkness.

"Wait for me!" yelled Tom.

It was colder and pitch-black inside the second chamber. Jamie aimed his flashlight at the rock walls, ceiling, and floor. There was no sign of any soot from smugglers' lamps.

"We must be the first people to come in here for hundreds of years," Tom murmured.

"Thousands of years!" said Jamie.

"Millions!" said Tom.

"Hey, what's this?" The beam of Jamie's flashlight fell on a scoop in the stone next to his feet. He kneeled down and traced his finger around the clover-shaped indent. It looked just like the dinosaur footprint on his Fossil Finder.

"I think this could be a fossil," Jamie announced, excitement tingling through him.

Jamie rummaged in his bag and flipped open the Fossil Finder. The display picture of a dinosaur footprint glowed in the darkness. "Yes, it's a fossilized dinosaur footprint!"

"Wow," Tom said, looking from the screen to the cave floor. "Those are really rare!"

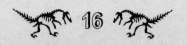

Jamie saw a second scoop at the edge of the beam of light. "Look! There's another . . . and another . . . five altogether. They go straight into that wall of rock."

Jamie could hardly believe it. On his very first day exploring Dinosaur Cove, he had found the fossilized tracks of a dinosaur!

Jamie carefully placed his left foot into the first print. "It's got the same size feet as me!" He swung his right foot into the next print. Jamie grinned at Tom, who was following behind him. "We're tracking dinosaurs! Left foot."

A crack of light appeared in the cave wall.

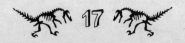

"Right foot . . ." The light brightened as the crack widened. Jamie put his left foot forward to take another step and the crack of light got wider and brighter. He covered his eyes with his hands. When he put his foot down again, the ground felt spongy.

Cautiously, he took his hands away from his eyes.

Jamie wasn't in the small dark chamber anymore. He was in a sunny cave with a wall of stone behind him. The footprints were still there — only now they weren't fossils. They were fresh!

He took a step forward into the new cave, and Tom appeared behind him — right through the wall of stone!

"Where are we?" Tom asked.

"I don't know," Jamie said, looking around at the strange new place.

Jamie walked out of the cave and the ground

squelched beneath his feet. The area was
thick with trees and vines, so he couldn't see
very far.

"These trees are weird."
Jamie pulled an apricot-like
fruit from a cluster hanging
on a nearby branch. It smelled horrible.
"Yuck! Dare you to smell it, Tom."

Tom took a huge sniff. "Sick!" he gasped.
Then he grinned. "Dare you to take a bite."

"No way!" said Jamie, shaking his head.

The ground was slimy from the stinky
orange outer pulp of the fruit that had fallen
off the tree. Jamie picked a fan-shaped leaf from
the tree. "You know, I think I've seen this some-
where before."

He dug out the Fossil Finder and typed *FAN-SHAPED LEAF*. The next moment, pictures of leaves appeared on the screen. Jamie clicked on the one that looked the same as the leaf in his hand.

GINKGO: A LIVING FOSSIL, he read to Tom. *STILL FOUND TODAY, BUT EVERYWHERE IN DINOSAUR TIMES; SOMETIMES KNOWN AS A STINK BOMB TREE.*

"Too right," said Tom. "Let's get some fresh air!" He pushed aside a tangle of vines. "What's through here?"

"Wait for me!" Jamie hurriedly sealed a few

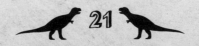

ginkgo fruits into a plastic specimen bag, stuffed them and the Fossil Finder into his backpack, and then crashed through the undergrowth after Tom.

"Careful!" Tom shouted to him from up ahead.

The ground sloped steeply and Jamie tried to slow down, but his sneakers were caked with slippery ginkgo pulp!

"I can't stop!" Jamie yelled as he tumbled toward the edge of the cliff.

CHAPTER 3

Tom thrust out the end of a stick. "Grab this, Jamie!" he shouted.

Jamie threw out his arm and caught hold as one foot went over the edge. He wobbled, and then steadied himself. "Thanks! That was close!"

Jamie stepped back from the cliff's edge and gazed at the landscape in front of him. A canopy of gray mist hung over a forest of brilliant emerald green. The humid air throbbed with the whirring and buzzing of insects.

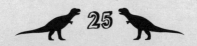

"Where is this?" he gasped. Among the trees, Jamie saw a beautiful blue lagoon and beyond that was an expanse of water. "Is that Dinosaur Cove?"

"No way," said Tom, looking through his binoculars. "That's an ocean."

Ark! Ark! Ark!

The sudden noise came out of the sky behind them and Jamie turned to see a scarlet-headed bird the size of a small airplane swooping toward them.

"Watch out!" he yelled to Tom.

They ducked as silver-gray leathery wings swept right over their heads. Tom followed the bird with his binoculars.

"It's flying over the jungle . . . it's settling on a tree by the lagoon," he told Jamie. "Take a look! It's huge!"

He thrust the binoculars at Jamie. Jamie looked toward the lagoon and his jaw dropped open. He couldn't believe his eyes!

"What can you see?" Tom asked.

"I can see," Jamie spoke carefully, "two rhinos, but instead of one big horn, they have three. Which means," he whispered, "that they're not rhinos . . . they're triceratops!"

"What?" Tom said. "Let me see!"

Jamie passed the binoculars back. "You're right," Tom said. "And that huge bird isn't a bird at all. It's a pterodactyl!"

The boys looked at each other in amazement.

"DINOSAURS!!"

they yelled together, punching the air.

"But how . . . ?" Tom stuttered.

"I don't know," yelled Jamie. "But we've got to get closer!"

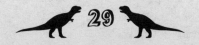

"Over there," said Tom. "There's a slope down to the jungle."

The boys scrambled and skidded down the hill, and soon their feet sank into the spongy jungle floor. Great pine trees towered above them and huge ferns brushed damply against their legs as they passed. An enormous frill of purple and yellow spotted fungus caught Jamie's eye. It sprouted from a rotten tree stump.

"This is unreal!" Jamie said. But then, on the far side of the fungus, the ferns began to rustle.

Grunk.

"Did you hear that?" Jamie whispered.

"What?" Tom stood still.

The ferns swished. *Grunk.*

"That!" Jamie hissed. "There's something there!"

Jamie and Tom ducked down behind the tree stump, and then slowly peeked out from behind the fungus.

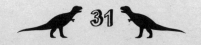

The noises were coming from a plump, scaly creature with a flat, bony head and splotchy green-brown markings. It was standing on two strong legs, peering hopefully into a tree.

"It's a little dinosaur!" Jamie whispered.

As they watched, the little dinosaur grabbed hold of the pine tree with its claws, steadying itself by digging its long tail into the ground. Then it shook the tree as hard as its short arms would allow. The little dinosaur's tail twitched and it grunted softly to itself.

"He's thinking," Tom murmured.

"He's so cool!" Jamie breathed.

The dinosaur took a few steps back. He lowered his bony head and charged straight at the tree.

Thwack!

The flat top of the dinosaur's head hit the trunk and the pine tree shook.

"He's strong," said Tom.

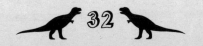

32

Thwack!

"Do you think he's dangerous?" Jamie asked.

"I'll look him up." Tom pulled the Fossil Finder out of Jamie's backpack, and tapped in keywords: *FLAT SKULL, HEAD BUTT.*

WAN-NA-NO-SAUR-US, Tom read from the screen. *A HERBIVORE.*

"That means a plant eater," added Jamie.

USES ITS HARD SKULL TO DEFEND ITSELF AGAINST PREDATORS, Tom continued.

As Tom slipped the Fossil Finder back into Jamie's bag, the little dinosaur took another run up and rammed the tree again.

"He thinks the tree's a predator!" Tom stood up, laughing.

At the sound of Tom's laughter, the little dinosaur cocked his head to one side. He turned and blinked mournfully at Tom.

"You've hurt his feelings," Jamie said, standing up beside Tom.

"Sorry, Wanna," Tom apologized to the little dinosaur.

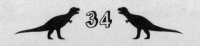

The wannanosaurus blinked at Tom and then at Jamie. He took three big steps away from the tree and shifted his weight from foot to foot.

"He's revving up," said Jamie.

"Go, Wanna, go!" the boys shouted.

The wannanosaurus put his head down and hurtled toward the tree.

Thwack!

The tree wobbled.

Plunk!

A single pine cone dropped to the ground. The dinosaur stuffed it into his mouth and looked happily at the boys. Then he wagged his tail and scurried off on his hind legs.

"Let's track him!" said Tom.

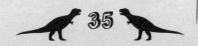

35

"Just a minute . . ." Jamie carved a w into the tree stump with his fossil hammer. "So we remember where we met Wanna."

"Now, which way did he go?" asked Jamie as they clambered over the tree.

Tom looked around at the trampled plants. "He disturbs the ferns as he walks on them," Tom said. "We can follow his trail."

The little dinosaur's trail led to a small clearing where the boys found him standing on his hind legs, munching a leaf. He turned toward them and lowered his flat bony head.

"Uh-oh," said Tom. "He might charge us!"

"It's OK, Wanna. We're not predators." Jamie put his backpack on the ground and took out his bag of stinky ginkgo fruit. He rolled one toward the wannanosaurus. The dinosaur sniffed at the fruit suspiciously.

"He can't possibly want to eat that," said Tom, holding his nose.

Wanna looked down his snout at Tom, then

he pinned the fruit
between his claws and
sank his teeth into it.
He made grunking noises as
stinky ginkgo juice dribbled down
his chin.

"Yum yum!" Jamie grimaced as the
dinosaur's long tongue slurped up every
disgusting drop.

Wanna looked at Jamie. Then he looked
at Jamie's backpack and wagged his tail.

Suddenly, the little dinosaur froze.

The jungle went still. Even the
insects stopped buzzing. The ground
trembled beneath their feet.

"Something's coming," whispered
Jamie. "Something big . . ."

CHAPTER 4

*T*hump!

The ground shook. Wanna dashed behind the leafy tree.

Thump!

A stronger tremor shook the ground. Wanna peeped out from behind a branch and bobbed his head up and down.

In the distance, wood was snapping and cracking. The tremors were getting stronger.

"Whatever it is, is coming our way," Jamie said.

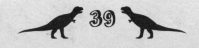

"Fast," added Tom.

The boys looked at each other.

"We've got to get out of here!" Jamie yelled.

"Which way?"

Suddenly, Jamie's bag was yanked off his back. Jamie spun around and saw Wanna

charging off into the jungle, clutching it in his mouth.

"Wanna!" Jamie sprinted after him, Tom close behind.

The little dinosaur skidded to a halt by a shallow stream. He turned and looked Jamie in the eyes. Then he jerked his head toward the stream and plunged in.

The ground shook again.

"Wanna's leading us to safety!" Jamie shouted, jumping into the stream after him.

"Clever!" Tom panted. "The water will mask our scent."

Wanna led them up the stream to where it trickled through a jumble of huge, rounded rocks. He glanced back and leaped out of the water.

Jamie and Tom followed, stumbling and splashing. They scrambled onto the rocks and stood, dripping.

"Where's he gone?" Jamie asked.

RAAAR!

Something crashed through the trees behind them. Jamie whirled around and lost his footing on the wet stones.

Tom threw out his hand, but when Jamie grabbed it, both boys toppled and slid down between two rocks. Jamie landed with a thud

and found himself
staring into a reptilian face.

Grunk!

Wanna greeted Jamie and
Tom with slobbery licks,
and Jamie was happy to see
his backpack again.

"Are we safe?" Jamie
whispered. "Is that thing
chasing us gone?"

The boys listened.

"I think so!" Tom
breathed.

Thud!

The rocks shook.

"It's here!" Tom whispered.

Jamie peered up through the
gap above his head. Instead of
the trees of the jungle, he saw a
dark slimy hole.

Suddenly, a blast of slime flew from

the hole and splattered
Jamie's face.

"*Aargh!*" Jamie wiped
his face. "I think that's
its nose."

The creature lifted its head
and roared.

RAAAR!

The sound rumbled around the rocks.

Jamie could see its jaws. Slithers of rotting
flesh dangled from its fangs.

"*Ugh*! Bad breath!" Jamie gagged. "Worse
than stinky ginkgo fruit."

"It doesn't look friendly," Tom said. "W-what
is it?"

An enormous yellow eye, rimmed with
bright red scales, studied Jamie through the gap
in the rocks.

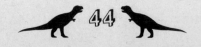

44

"D-don't n-need the F-Fossil Finder," Jamie stammered. "It's a

T-T-T-Rex!"

CHAPTER 5

SEARCH:

A B C D E F G H I J K L M N
O P Q R S T U V W X Y Z Shift
1 2 3 4 5 6 7 8 9 0 : ; " ` *

The eye disappeared.

"We're in trouble!" Jamie hissed.

"*Serious* trouble," Tom said.

Suddenly, a long claw stabbed down into the crevice.

"Watch out!" Jamie yelled. He pulled Tom back and thrust his bag out as a shield. Wanna and Tom shrank back behind it.

The claw scratched and scrabbled around the gap in the rocks.

"It can't get us!" Tom whispered. "Its arms are too short."

"Maybe it will go away now," Jamie said. But the huge unblinking eye of the T-Rex reappeared.

Wanna trembled.

"If I had a stick," Tom muttered. "I'd poke it in the eye!"

"There must be something we can use." Jamie groped in his backpack. "Let's see how it likes this." Jamie pulled out his flashlight and aimed it at the T-Rex's eye. He flicked it on.

RAAAR!

The eye vanished. Cautiously, Jamie poked his head out of the crevice. The T-Rex was stomping away into the jungle.

"Whew!" Jamie said. "I think we're safe."

The boys gave each other a high five.

"Now, let's get out of here," Tom said. "Before it comes back!"

The boys and the little dinosaur climbed out of the crevice, and Wanna took the lead again, heading further downstream. "Did you see that thing's teeth?" Jamie muttered as they splashed after their new dinosaur friend. "That T-Rex could rip us to shreds!"

Tom shuddered. "And eat us alive, bit by bit!"

Gradually, the stream grew wider and the trees on either side began to thin out. Soon, the boys had come to the edge of the blue lagoon that they had seen earlier from Ginkgo Hill. Wanna stopped near a large rock and began to munch on a leafy bush.

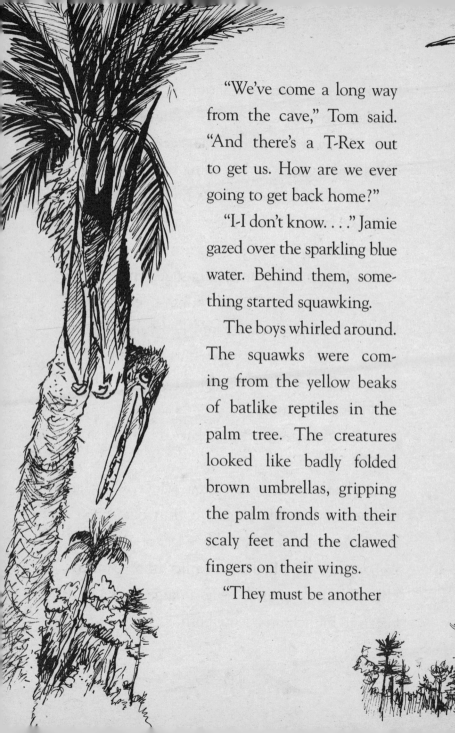

"We've come a long way from the cave," Tom said. "And there's a T-Rex out to get us. How are we ever going to get back home?"

"I-I don't know. . . ." Jamie gazed over the sparkling blue water. Behind them, something started squawking.

The boys whirled around. The squawks were coming from the yellow beaks of batlike reptiles in the palm tree. The creatures looked like badly folded brown umbrellas, gripping the palm fronds with their scaly feet and the clawed fingers on their wings.

"They must be another

type of
pterodactyl,"
Tom decided.

Just then, the ptero-
dactyls launched
themselves into the
air, squawking and
flapping their wings.

"What's up with them?" Tom asked
as the bird-like creatures flew away.

The lagoon fell silent. The only sound was
the water gently lapping on the shore. Then the
ground began to shake.

"Uh-oh," Jamie and Tom said together.

"T-Rex!"

CHAPTER 6

The boys turned to see the T-Rex spring out of the jungle, sending up a spray of sand. Its green scales rippled in the sunshine as it scanned the beach.

Then, it saw them.

RAAAR!

The T-Rex lowered its head. The red crests over its eyes flashed as it stomped toward them.

"We're T-Rex food," moaned Tom.

Then, suddenly, there was
a sound of breaking branches behind them.
The T-Rex's head snapped up and it stared at
the edge of the jungle.

Turning around slowly, Jamie saw a second
T-Rex crash out of the trees onto the beach.

"Oh no!" said Tom.

It was as big as the first, but darker, with black
stripes. And it was advancing on them.

"Watch out!" Jamie rolled out of the way of a huge foot as the first T-Rex stomped to meet the other T-Rex.

Tom ducked as its tail swept over his head.

The boys watched as the first T-Rex hurled itself at the newcomer.

"They're not after us!" he breathed.

"Maybe they're fighting over territory," Tom guessed.

The first T-Rex sank its jaws into the other's throat. The dark T-Rex screeched and writhed and thrashed its tail. Then it broke free, and sprang onto the first T-Rex's back. It hung on, biting its neck.

"Let's get out of here! Run!" Jamie dragged Tom toward the trees. Wanna bounded after them.

Gradually, the snarls and roars of the T-Rex battle faded into the jungle sounds.

"We're lost, aren't we?" Tom sat down on the ground and put his head in his hands. "How are we going to get back?"

Grunk . . . *grunk* . . . grunk . . .

Wanna darted off into the trees.

"Maybe we could follow Wanna?" Jamie said. "It's our best chance."

After a moment, they were back at a stream. "Is this the same stream as before?" Jamie wondered.

Next, Wanna led them through a jumble of rounded rocks.

"That's where we hid from the T-Rex!" Tom remembered.

They passed the purple and yellow-spotted

fungus and Jamie bent down and saw the w on the tree stump. "The Wanna tree!" He grinned.

Then they climbed the slope through the ginkgo trees and, finally, they were standing in the mouth of the cave.

"That's how we got here!" Jamie pointed to the fresh dinosaur footprint by the solid rock wall.

Wanna stood next to it, and wagged his tail. Then he stepped away, leaving two more identical footprints, but this time facing the rock.

"They're your footprints!" Jamie gasped.

Wanna blinked at him, turned, and scurried into a pile of leaves and twigs in the corner of the cave.

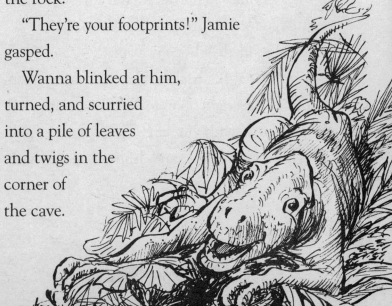

"That's Wanna's nest!" Jamie took out the last ginkgo fruit from his backpack.

"This is for you, Wanna," he said, putting it on the ground. "Thank you for helping us." Wanna's snout poked out of his nest. He nosed the fruit back to Jamie.

"I think he wants you to have it," Tom said.

"OK, Wanna," said Jamie, picking it up. "I'll put it in Dad's museum," he told Tom, screwing up his nose and smiling.

Tom was gazing at the rock with a puzzled expression on his face. "We stepped forward to go back in time, so maybe we have to step backward to go forward in time," he guessed.

Jamie nodded. "I hope it works!"

Tom turned his back to the rock face. Then he placed his right foot in Wanna's print and stepped back with his left. There was a flash of light and Jamie found himself alone with Wanna.

"It worked!" Jamie said to Wanna. "That means we can come back and see you again!"

He patted the little dinosaur on the snout. Wanna licked Jamie's hand, then curled up in his nest.

"Good-bye, Wanna!" Jamie held the ginkgo fruit in one hand and his flashlight in the other. As he stepped back through the blaze of light, he felt the ground turn to stone beneath his feet. Then, he was back in the cave with Tom.

Jamie felt the ginkgo fruit in his hand soften. In the flashlight beam, he watched it shrivel and crumble to dust.

"We can't bring anything back," he told Tom, letting the dust trickle between his fingers.

"It's just as well," Tom said. "That thing stank."

The boys squeezed through the hole in the rock, scrambled down the boulders, and hurried down the cliff path onto the beach.

Jamie's grandfather was packing up his fishing gear. He smiled at the boys as he reeled in his fishing line.

"Did you find any dinosaurs?" he asked them.

Jamie winked at Tom. "We found an awesome cave, didn't we, Tom?"

"Awesome!" agreed Tom. "Let's explore it some more tomorrow!"

"Great idea!" said Jamie, hoisting up his backpack, and turning to his Grandpa. "If that's OK with you and Dad?"

"Just as long as you're not getting into any trouble. . . ." His eyes twinkled as he slung his fishing rod over his shoulder and picked up his bucket of fish.

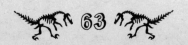

"See you tomorrow, Tom?" Jamie said to his new friend.

"Sure thing!" Tom said as he waved good-bye.

Jamie and his grandpa walked back up the path to the old lighthouse. His grandfather asked, "You think you'll like living around here then?"

"Definitely!" said Jamie with a grin. "I can't wait to explore more of Dinosaur Cove!"

GLOSSARY

Ammonite – an extinct animal with octopus-like legs and often a spiral-shaped shell that lived in the ocean

Conifer – cone-bearing trees such as pines or cedars

Fossil – the remains or imprint of plants or animals found in rocks. They help scientists unravel the mysteries of prehistoric times.

Ginkgo – a tree native to China called a "living fossil" because fossils of it have been found dating back millions of years, yet they are still around today. Also known as the stink bomb tree because of its smelly apricot-like fruit.

Herbivore – an animal that only eats plants; a vegetarian

Lagoon – a body of water, like a lake, that is separated from a larger body of water, like an ocean, by a barrier of coral or sand

Pterodactyl – a flying prehistoric reptile which could be as small as a bird or as large as an airplane

Triceratops (T-Tops) – a three-horned, plant-eating dinosaur which looked like a rhinoceros

Tyrannosaurus Rex (T-Rex) – a meat-eating dinosaur with a huge tail, two strong legs, but two tiny arms. T-Rex was one of the biggest and scariest dinosaurs.

Wannanosaurus – a dinosaur that only ate plants and used its hard, flat skull to defend itself. Named after the place it was discovered: Wannano in China.

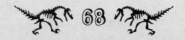

LOOK OUT!
HERE I COME ...

TRICERATOPS STAMPEDE!

Thrill-seeking Tom leads Jamie into the middle of a herd of triceratops on the move. Will Jamie come up with a brilliant solution, or will the three-horned giants crush their hopes of escape?